Dad stopped the car
at a camping ground by a lake.

Katie and Joe were staying with him
for the holidays.

"This looks like a good place
for camping," said Joe.
"We can go swimming and fishing."

The Secret Cave

Story by Annette Smith
Illustrations by Meredith Thomas

"Look at that notice!" said Katie.
"There is a secret cave
   down that track!   Can we go now?"

"No, Katie," said Dad.
"We have to put the tent up first.
   Remember, you are not to go away
   by yourself."

Joe helped Dad put the tent up.
Katie helped to get the bags
and other things out of the car.
They all worked hard.

Then Dad said to Joe,
"Where is Katie?"

"She's not in here," said Joe,
looking in the tent.
"And she's not in the car."

Joe and Dad looked everywhere
but they couldn't find Katie.

"I hope she didn't go down that track
by herself to find the cave," said Dad.
"We had better go and see."

"It will be getting dark, soon,"
said Joe.

Katie **had** gone down the track.
She had gone off by herself
to find the secret cave.
The track was wet and muddy.

After Katie had walked a little way,
she found the cave
by the side of the track.
Katie looked inside.
It was dark.
But then she saw something.

11

Just then, Dad and Joe
came running along the track.
"**Katie!**" cried Dad.

"We have been looking everywhere
for you," said Joe.

"I'm sorry," said Katie.
"I was just going to walk a little way
down the track.
Look! I have found the **cave**.
Come and see!
There's a secret inside it!"

They went inside the cave.

"Look at the little lights
all over the walls," said Katie.

"Sh-sh-sh!" said Dad.
"They are glow-worms.
They have little lights
on the ends of their tails.
We must be very quiet
or they will put their lights out."

"The glow-worms are a good secret,"
said Katie.
"Can we come and see them again?"

"Yes, Katie," said Dad, giving her a hug.
"But remember, you must not go away
 by yourself again. You did scare me."

"I'm sorry, Dad," said Katie.
"I won't forget."